Grandma's Band

written by Brad Bowles
designed and illustrated by
Anthony Chan

Stemmer House
PUBLISHERS, INC.
OWINGS MILLS, MARYLAND

Inquiries should be directed to
Stemmer House Publishers, Inc.
2627 Caves Road
Owings Mills, Maryland 21117

A Barbara Holdridge book

Printed and bound in Hong Kong

First Edition 1989

Library of Congress Cataloging-in-Publication Data

Bowles, Brad, 1943-
    Grandma's band/written by Brad Bowles; designed and illustrated
by Anthony Chan.—1st ed.
      p. cm.
    "A Barbara Holdridge book"—T.p. verso.
    Summary: Grandma's enthusiastic one-woman washboard band
captivates a number of neighboring animals and leads them to join
her in making music.
    ISBN 0-88045-112-2: $14.95
    [1. Bands (Music)—Fiction.   2. Animals—Fiction.] I. Chan,
Anthony, ill. II. Title.
PZ7.B6788Gr 1989
[E]—dc20
                                        89-36217
                                        CIP
                                        AC

Grandma's Band

For my father,
E. J. Bowles

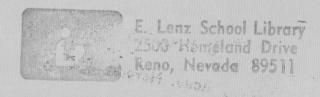

Grandma was tired and bored.

It was almost nine o'clock in the morning, and she'd been washing clothes on her old washboard for a while.

She was sitting out there on the front porch wishing she could be doing anything else but washing that huge pile of dirty clothes.

Now earlier that morning, Grandma had forgotten to take the thimble off her finger when she finished darning her grandson's socks. And now, while she was scrubbing a very dirty shirt, that finger with the thimble on it slipped off the shirt and ran right across the metal part of the washboard— "diddle diddle diddle diddle diddle diddle diddle!"— like a stick dragged along a picket fence, only louder.

Grandma jumped. She was surprised. She tried again—"diddle diddle diddle!" She smiled. Again and again—"diddle diddle" and "diddle diddle." She giggled. And then she tried it a whole bunch of times—"diddle diddle diddle diddle diddle" and "diddle diddle diddle diddle diddle!"—and she laughed.

She kept pulling that thimble over her washboard, over and over and over—one, *two, three, four*—and her foot started tapping in time with that happy washboard sound.

She remembered dancing with Grandpa at those old-timey barn dances she went to on Saturday nights long ago. And then she recalled jumping rope even longer ago, when she was a little girl in the schoolyard.

She even started chanting in time to
the beat:

> **Johnny on the ocean,**
> **Johnny on the sea,**
> **Johnny broke a teacup**
> **and blamed it on me.**

"Yeah, yeah, yeah!" she said out loud. And she
remembered some more:

> **I told ma and ma told pa,**
> **Johnny got a lickin'—hee haw, hee haw.**
> **Salt, vinegar, mustard, PEPPER!**

Grandma forgot all about the dirty clothes. She looked up and saw an old tin water cup sitting on the railing of the porch. She reached up and tapped it. "Bing!!" And she tried again: "Bing, bing, bing, bing!"

Then she had an idea.

She went inside the house and got another thimble, two pots, two pans, three canning jars, and the lid to an old iron pot. She hurried back to the porch, put on the other thimble, and started banging and beating all those pots and things and running her fingers over the washboard.

She started singing:

You get a line and
I'll get a pole, honey.
You get a line and
I'll get a pole, babe.
You get a line and
I'll get a pole and
We'll go down to the
crawdad hole.
Honey, oh baby, mine.

Now there was a duck who lived on a little pond in the woods east of Grandma's house. Duck heard Grandma singing and banging away. So she swam to the shore of the pond and waddled westward. Then she got a running start and—*pheeoo!*—took off and flew out over the house and saw Grandma down there making noise to beat the band. Why Grandma *was* the band.

Duck landed to get a better look. She listened. She liked what she heard. She moved a little closer. And a little closer. And with each waddle, she liked Grandma's noise a lot better. And when she was just a few feet away, she started singing along—*"Quack, quack, quackity quack."*

Grandma froze. Duck froze. She stared right at Grandma.

Well, Grandma smiled, and, although it is hard to know when a duck is smiling—through that beak and all—it seemed like that duck was smiling too. Grandma rolled her thimble over the washboard. Duck cocked her head to one side. Grandma tapped on the tin cup. Duck's eyes opened up real wide. Grandma tapped a pot and a pan and a fruit jar, all in a little rhythm. Duck started tapping her little webbed foot and swaying back and forth in time to the beat.

Then Grandma started singing—

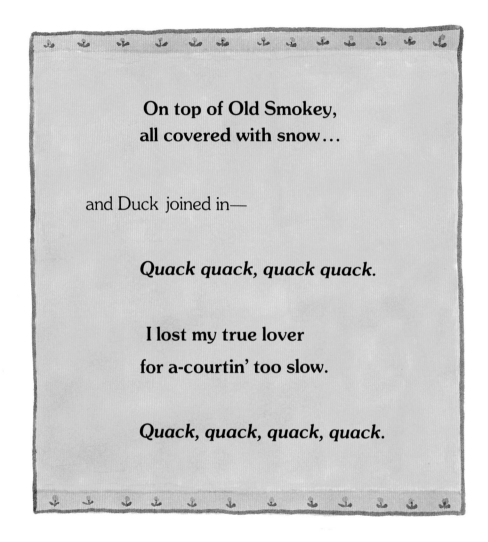

On top of Old Smokey,
all covered with snow...

and Duck joined in—

Quack quack, quack quack.

I lost my true lover
for a-courtin' too slow.

Quack, quack, quack, quack.

There they were, Grandma and Duck. And
they made a pretty good duet. Yes, they did.

Now up in the barn there was a cow who had been trying to chew her cud in peace. But with all that noise, she couldn't. So, she wandered on out of the barn and stopped to listen. And the more she listened, the more she liked what she heard. She started tapping along with one of her front hooves, and, after a minute, *she* joined in the singing:

I lost my true lover,

Moo moo, moo moo.

For acourtin' too slow.

Quack quack, moo moo.

Without missing a note, Grandma looked out at the cow and smiled. Duck smiled. And Cow smiled right back. They kept on making happy music, and it got better and better and louder and louder.

So loud, in fact, that a hungry red fox who lived in the woods heard that mooing and quacking and singing and clacking. And the sound of that quacking reminded him how much he liked ducks to eat, especially for breakfast.

He tippy-toed out of the woods through the tall grass and stopped to listen. He moved closer and closer, and as he did, the spell of the happy music came over him. He let out a little yelping noise—"yip"—right in time with the singing. Well, that stopped everything. Duck fluttered up onto the porch and hid behind Grandma's skirts. She was shaking. Grandma stood up and put her hands on her hips and stared down at Fox. Cow just turned her head toward Fox and chewed cud. Fox was frozen in his tracks.

After a moment of stillness, Grandma thought that this fox didn't seem like he meant any harm. Cow wasn't scared. Duck had stopped shaking. So she decided to play her washboard again. In a minute old Cow was twitching her tail, and Duck was waddling a little. And Fox—everybody was keeping at least one eye on that red fox—well, he started wagging his tail in time with the beat. Grandma tried another song:

**She'll be comin' 'round
the mountain when she comes.**

and Red Fox yipped *"Yip, yip."*

**She'll be comin' 'round
the mountain when she comes.**

Quack quack.

**She'll be comin' 'round
the mountain,
she'll be comin' 'round
the mountain,
she'll be comin' 'round
the mountain when she comes.**

Quack quack, moo moo, yip yip!

So, at that very moment, Red Fox became a member of Grandma's band. Sounded pretty good, too. So good, in fact, they kept getting louder and louder.

Someone else heard them.

Old Mother Hen had been trying to lay her
Saturday morning egg up in the chicken coop. But
with all the merrymaking, she couldn't.

She skittered out into the yard, and when
she saw Grandma's quartet having so much fun,
she forgot all about her egg and started plucking away
at the top of her scratchy little voice.

She'll be comin' 'round
the mountain when she comes.
Quack quack, moo moo, yip yip,
puh-luckity-pluck!

And every once in a while she'd flap her wings
in time with the beat. Nice touch.

Now all this time there was a great big, old,

hairy, hungry, toothy wolf hanging around out near

the woods watching and listening to Grandma and

her friends.

He was planning out his menu for the

week: "Duck on Monday, chicken on Tuesday,

and Grandma on Wednesday,

Thursday

and Friday."

He started sneaking up on them through the tall grass—real low to the ground, like a furry snake. And when he got close, he jumped up out of the grass, growled his loudest growl, and ran full speed out into the yard, trying to look as mean and scary as he could.

And as that old wolf was coming right at them, teeth shining in the sun, Old Mama Hen flew up above the wolf, and laid her Saturday morning egg…right on his head! Wolf stopped dead still. Duck flew up over him, landed right on his hairy shoulders and began to flap her wings as hard as she could in his ears. And Red Fox began to run around and around and around that old wolf as fast as he could, faster and faster. Wolf started to get real dizzy. And just as soon as he was about to fall over, Old Cow backed up to him and twitched her tail in his nose. And Old Wolf…"Ah…ah…ah…choooo!" sneezed!

Now, all that old wolf wanted to do was get out of there. But how could he? He could hardly see, he could barely stand up. So he just sat down and whimpered like a little bitty puppy dog. Hung his head and whimpered.

Grandma got up real slowly, stepped down off the porch, walked up to the wolf and said: "Get on out of here, you old wolf. Go on now."

Wolf stood up, his eyes pretty sad, with his tail between his legs, and began to slink off toward the woods.

After he had gotten almost out of sight,
Grandma and her friends started making their music
again.

I went to the animal fair.
Quack quack.
The birds and beasts were there.
Moo moo.
The old racoon
in the light of the moon
was combing his tangled hair.
Yip yip.
The monkey saw a skunk.
Pluck pluck.
He climbed up the elephant's trunk.
Yippity yip.
The elephant sneezed
and fell to his knees,
and what became of the monk?
Moo moo, yippity-yip,
puh-luckity-pluck,
quack quack!

Wolf stopped. Wolf listened. He began to like what he was hearing. He turned around. He watched Grandma's happy band. Grandma was smiling and singing, duck was quacking and waddling, old cow mooing and flicking her tail, red fox yipping along, and old mother hen was plucking away. And do you know what? That old wolf wished …well, he wished that he could join in the fun, even though he knew they'd never trust him again.

But the spell of the music was just too much. He *had* to try it. He let out a little howl—*"Whooooo."* And another—*"Whooooo!"* And another—*"Whooooo!"*

The sound of those howls carried on the wind right on down to Grandma and her band. They heard those howls and, after a minute, they began to like them. Yes, they did.

"Clackity quack, moo, yip yip, pluckity pluck" and *"whooooo! whooooo!"*

Old Wolf began to edge on back toward the farmhouse, real slow, all the time howling in time with the rest. As he got closer and closer, he felt better and better. And the music started sounding sweeter and sweeter. And in a moment, everybody felt it. Their music had never sounded so good.

By the time the old wolf had gotten pretty close to the porch, Grandma was smiling, so wolf sat right down and began to howl like he'd never howled before—and it sounded like singing. It did. It fit right in with all the other voices.

"Clackity quack, moo, yip yip, pluckity pluck" and *"whooooo! whooooo!"*

Well, they kept on making music until way after noon, until all of them were too tired and too full of happy feelings to play and sing anymore.

So they all went back to where they were before Grandma had discovered music in her washboard, with no bad feelings, only good ones. And Grandma used that washboard to finish washing the clothes. She didn't mind that now at all.

And every Saturday morning about nine o'clock, Grandma and all her friends come together around the porch—duck and cow and fox and hen *and* wolf—and sing and play and pluck and quack and clack and yip and moo and whooooo—until they are all as happy as can be.

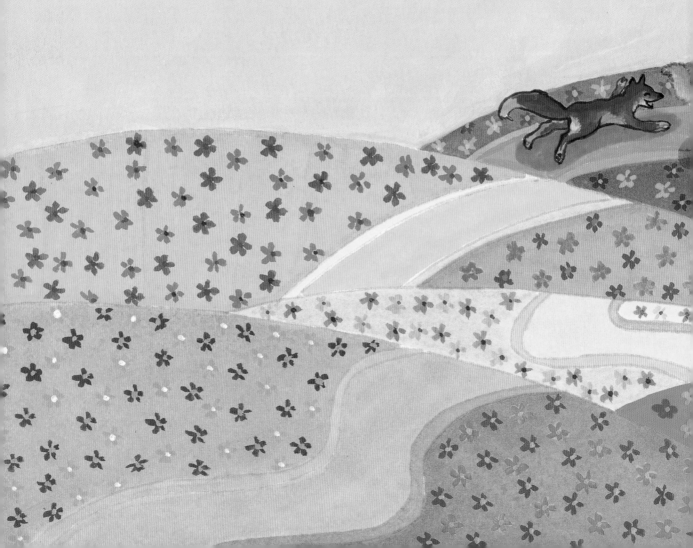

The monkey saw a skunk.
Pluck pluck.
He climbed up the elephant's trunk.
Yippity yip.
The elephant sneezed and
fell to his knees and what
became of the monk?

Moo moo, yippity-yip,
puh-luckity-pluck,
clackity-quack,
whooooo! whooooo!

Every Saturday morning.

Yes, they do.

Colophon

Designed by Anthony Chan and Barbara Holdridge

Composed in Souvenir Light and Medium by Brown Composition
Company, Baltimore, Maryland, with Fox display

Jacket color separations by GraphTec, Baltimore, Maryland

Printed on 85-pound acid-free matte paper and bound by
Everbest Printing Company, Hong Kong/Four Colour Imports, Ltd.,
Louisville, Kentucky